Adapted by Lee Howard
Interior illustrated by Alcadia Snc
Cover illustrated by Duendes del Sur
Based the episode "3-D Destruction" by Ed Scharlach

ISBN 978-0-545-50186-6

12 11 10 9 8 7 6 5 4 3 2   13 14 15 16 17/0

Original design by Kara Kenna
Revised design by Cheung Tai
Printed in the U.S.A   40
First printing, January 2013

SCHOLASTIC INC.

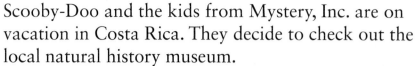

Scooby-Doo and the kids from Mystery, Inc. are on vacation in Costa Rica. They decide to check out the local natural history museum.

THIS MUSEUM IS FAMOUS FOR ITS WORK ON DINOSAUR FOSSILS AND BONES.

I'M THE MUSEUM CURATOR, DR. GUTIERREZ. I HOPE YOU ENJOY OUR DINOSAUR EXHIBIT.

Next, the gang meets Melbourne O'Reilly, a legendary fossil hunter.

G'DAY, MATES.

WOW, IT'S AN HONOR TO MEET YOU! I JUST SAW YOUR PICTURE ON A MAGAZINE COVER. YOU WERE HAND-CATCHING PIRANHAS IN THE AMAZON RIVER!

Heather leads the gang around the museum. First stop, moon rocks!

WE'RE ONE OF THE FEW MUSEUMS TO EXHIBIT REAL MOON ROCKS. THAT'S THE EXCAVATOR THE ASTRONAUTS USED TO RECOVER THEM.

Next, she takes the gang on a tour of the old mineshaft. Then it's back to the auditorium for a special presentation.

Dr. Gutierrez introduces a new documentary about dinosaurs.

That's because this dino is for real! Scooby and the gang run for their lives.

Fortunately, everyone manages to escape unharmed. But the museum's exhibits aren't so lucky. . . .

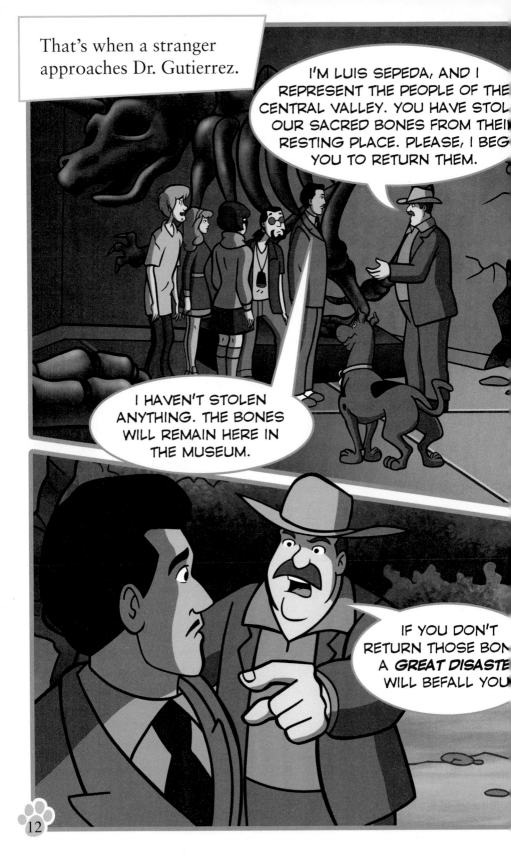

That's when a stranger approaches Dr. Gutierrez.

I'M LUIS SEPEDA, AND I REPRESENT THE PEOPLE OF THE CENTRAL VALLEY. YOU HAVE STOL OUR SACRED BONES FROM THEI RESTING PLACE. PLEASE, I BEG YOU TO RETURN THEM.

I HAVEN'T STOLEN ANYTHING. THE BONES WILL REMAIN HERE IN THE MUSEUM.

IF YOU DON'T RETURN THOSE BON A *GREAT DISASTE* WILL BEFALL YOU

Melbourne O'Reilly brings the gang back to the mine to look for the dinosaur.

THE FOOTPRINTS LEAD THIS WAY.

Shaggy steps into a puddle of goop.

I THINK IT'S DINOSAUR DROOL, SHAGGY.

LIKE, WHAT?!

The next thing Shaggy finds is a lot less disgusting . . . gold!

The mine's tunnels branch off in three different directions.

WHICH WAY SHOULD WE GO?

LET'S SPLIT UP AND LOOK FOR CLUES.

I'LL TAKE THE FIRST TUNNEL.

Fred, Velma, and Daphne take the second tunnel. That leaves Scooby and Shaggy with the third.

The two buddies haven't gone far when they hear a rumbling sound. . . .

Now the dinosaur's got the whole gang cornered!

It's Shaggy and Scooby to the rescue Fred, Velma, and Daphne pile into the railroad cart.

The gang manages to outrun the dinosaur. They find an old exit that takes them to the jungle outside the museum.

AH! YOU MADE IT OUT SAFELY. I'M ALL RIGHT, TOO, MATES.

I'M PRETTY SURE THAT'S NOT A REAL DINOSAUR. BUT SOMEONE WANTS US TO BELIEVE IT IS. . . .

The kids head back inside to do a little more investigating.

ICK! YOU'RE TRACKING IN THAT DROOL WE FOUND EARLIER.

ISN'T THAT PROOF THERE'S A REAL DINOSAUR?

WAIT, I'VE SEEN THIS KIND OF STUFF BEFORE IT'S USED TO MAK COSMETICS.

Velma runs some of the suspects' pictures through face-recognition software.

WHAT ABOUT MELBOURNE O'REILLY? SEEMS LIKE HE WOULD DO ANYTHING TO BE A HERO.

Next she runs a picture of Señor Se

I HAVE A FUNN FEELING ABOUT T GUY AND HIS ANC CURSES. . . .

JEEPERS! ACCORDING TO INTERPOL, HE'S A CON MAN! HE'S WANTED FOR SELLING ANCIENT RELICS ON THE BLACK MARKET.

It's time for one of Fred's famous plans.

WE NEED SHAGGY AND SCOOBY TO LURE THE DINOSAUR OUT OF THE MINESHAFT.

The next thing Scooby and Shaggy know, they're waiting for the dinosaur to attack!

LIKE, WHY ARE WE ALWAYS THE ONES WHO END UP AS BAIT?

The plan works! The dinosaur follows Shaggy and Scooby out of the mine and into the jungle.

Then it crashes through the glass entrance and chases them into the museum!

Shaggy and Scooby lead the dinosaur straight to the dinosaur bones exhibit—and into Fred's trap!

Fred pulls a rope, and a huge skeleton crashes down on the dinosaur.

WAY TO GO, GUYS! WE'VE GOT HIM!

But Fred has underestimated the dinosaur's strength. The enormous creature flexes its back and breaks loose!

The dinosaur has disappeared again! But Velma has an idea. . . .

I THINK I'VE FIGURED IT OUT! LET'S GET EVERYONE TO COME BACK TO THE AUDITORIUM.

Once the audience is in their seats, Velma begins her slideshow.

SHAGGY AND I WENT BACK TO THE MINE AND DID A LITTLE EXPERIMENT. USING A SUBWOOFER, WE PROVED THAT THE ONLY LIVING CREATURES INSIDE THE MINE ARE BATS.

NO OTHER PERSON OR ANIMAL COULD ENDURE THIS SOUND.

GRRRR

Scooby agrees!